SPARKY'S BIG NEWS

BY NANCY LAPOINTE
ILLUSTRATED BY LEN HERNANDEZ
MOUSE TOWER PUBLICATIONS

Printed and bound in the United States of America

ISBN:

Hardback: 978-1-7356196-0-6

Paperback: 978-1-7356196-1-3

DEDICATIONS

From Nancy

To my beloved brother, Bobby, for sharing both the fun side of his gayness and the sorrows of his AIDS fight.

To my treasured son, Jett, for demonstrating what an integrity-driven life looks like. You inspire me.

To my beautiful daughters, Katie, Maggie, and Beth, for their laughter, love, and friendship.

To my love, John, for sharing his life with me.

From Len

For my talented and beautiful wife, Barb. Always by my side.

For my parents, Leo and Elva, and my brother, Chuck.

Always my rocks and in my heart.

For my friends. Always having my back.

For my babies, Ruby and Fuzz.

All my love.

I don't like playing soccer anymore, Mom. Some mean boys kick me in the shins and yell "Spaa-ky, Spaa-ky" and laugh at me.

I'll talk to the parents of the bullies. The taunting will stop. Please finish the season, and if you're still not having fun, choose another activity.

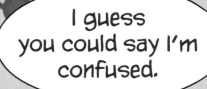

How do you leave home with one date and return with three?

Sparky is the best dancer ever! He danced with my friends and me all night. What an awesome prom!

ABOUT THE AUTHOR

Nancy Lapointe grew up wild and poor in small-town Mason City, Iowa. Stuck in a snowbank once too often, she migrated to South Texas, solo-parenting her four children.

Working as a bartender, high school English teacher, college adjunct professor, motivational speaker, and educational software developer, Lapointe financed her education, culminating in a doctoral degree in Educational Leadership from Texas A&M Corpus Christi/Kingsville.

Deemed controversial for her avant-garde teaching methods, Dr. Lapointe spent many hours in the principal's office. Finally, Harold E. Butt, grocery store magnate, validated her approach by naming her H-E-B Texas State Teacher of the Year. She tells other stories in her two novels, screenplay, and *Sparky's Big News*, a children's book with an important message about growing up gay.

Nancy celebrates her retirement in Escondido, California, fussing at her blue-eyed banditti grandsons and recycling vintage earrings. She and her loving partner, John Dinning, grow oranges in a forty-tree grove and force fruit on friends and food banks.

ABOUT THE ILLUSTRATOR

Len Hernandez, a San Antonio, Texas native, has lived and worked as a professional artist throughout the country. His credits include book illustrator and airbrush, portrait, and tattoo artist. His professional career spans thirty years. When he isn't creating art, Len is playing with his puppies, wrangling dolphins, watching *The Office*, or daydreaming about retiring on Kauai with his lovely wife, Barb. Hernandez loves himself a nice cup of coffee. *Mmmm*, coffee. And sharks—he loves sharks.